STEP INTO READING®

Two Princesses

By Bill Gordh

Illustrated by S.I. International

Random House New York

It was a dark and stormy night.
Barbie was snug in her bed.

She could hear the thunder
outside her window.

In ran Kelly and Stacie.
"Thunder scares me,"
said Kelly.

“Tell us a story, Barbie,”
said Stacie.
“You make up the best stories.”

Barbie looked around.

She saw a bunny.

She saw a big sparkly ring.

Bunny. Ring. Thunderstorm.

“Once upon a time,”
Barbie began,
“there were two princesses
named Kelly and Stacie . . .”

The two princesses
had magic rings.
The magic rings gave them
the power to talk to animals.

One day, the princesses wanted to have a picnic in the forest.

They filled a basket
with cheese, bread, carrots,
and nuts.

The two princesses
followed the river
to their picnic spot.

At last, they came
to Grand Oak, the biggest
tree in the forest.

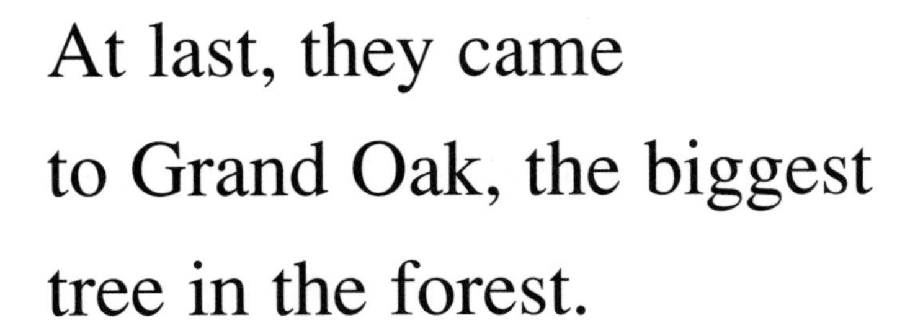

The birds were chirping.
The bunnies were hopping about.
There was enough picnic food
for everyone!

Suddenly, the princesses
felt raindrops.
Then it began to pour!

They took their basket
and ran for cover
inside Grand Oak.

The rain stopped.
The princesses came out.
They looked around.
Where was everyone?

A bunny hopped by.
"Bunny, wait!" Kelly cried.
"Where are you going?"

Bunny said,
"I have nowhere to go.
My house is filled
with rain water."

Just then Bird flew down.
"Tweet, tweet!" cried Bird.
"It rained so hard,
my nest fell out of the tree."

The two princesses looked at
each other.
They would help their friends.

"Bunny," said Kelly,
"we will help you dig
a new home."

Everyone went up the hill.
Stacie and Kelly dug
a nice new hole for Bunny.
"Thank you," said Bunny.

Kelly pointed to a tree.
"Bird," said Kelly,
"we will help you build
a new nest up there."

Everyone found twigs and
feathers and leaves.
They built a new nest.

Stacie climbed up the tree.
The nest was a good fit.
"Tweet, tweet!" said Bird.
"Thank you."

The two princesses
shared their picnic
with Bird and Bunny.

Stacie and Kelly smiled.
They loved helping
their friends.

Then it was time to go.
The princesses waved good-bye
and went back to their home.

"The end," said Barbie.

Kelly and Stacie looked up.

It was quiet outside.

"We like your story!"

said Kelly.

"And now," said Barbie,
"the storm is over.
That means it is time for
all princesses to go to bed!"